DINAMATION'S
DINOSAURS ALIVE!

First published in England in 1992 by Campbell Books
under the title DINAMATION'S DINOSAURS.

Text copyright © 1992 by Campbell Books.
Illustrations copyright © 1992 by Scholastic Inc.
Photographs copyright © 1992 by Dinamation International Corp.
All rights reserved. Published by Scholastic Inc.,
730 Broadway, New York, NY 10003,
by arrangement with Campbell Books.
CARTWHEEL BOOKS is a registered trademark of Scholastic Inc.
The use of the photographs in this book is licensed
by Dinamation International Corp.,
189-A Technology Drive, Irvine, CA 92718   Tel: 714-753-9630   Fax: 714-753-9657

Library of Congress Catalog Card Number: 92-82913

ISBN 0-590-47082-5

12 11 10 9 8 7 6 5 4 3 2 1   3 4 5 6 7 8/9

Printed in the U.S.A.   08

First Scholastic printing, November 1993

DINAMATION'S
DINOSAURS ALIVE!

Photographs by Dinamation International Corporation

SCHOLASTIC INC.

New York Toronto London Auckland Sydney

◄ INTRODUCTION ►

For more than 150 million years, Earth was home to all kinds of dinosaurs — huge dinosaurs and tiny dinosaurs, meat-eating dinosaurs and plant-eating dinosaurs, dinosaurs that walked on two legs and dinosaurs that walked on all four.

There were about 500 different types of dinosaurs, but they didn't all live at the same time. Some kinds died out before others appeared. The last dinosaurs died out long before there were any people on Earth.

How do we know about dinosaurs if nobody has ever seen one? Scientists dig up the fossil bones and teeth of dinosaurs and study them.

We know what these fascinating creatures looked like because experts have put together complete dinosaur skeletons. We know that dinosaur babies were hatched because their fossil eggs have been found.

The pictures in this book are photographs of moving dinosaur models. They show what scientists think these animals looked like and how they lived.

There are still some things we don't know about dinosaurs. We're not sure what colors they were or what sounds they made. We don't know exactly why they all died out. (Actually, a few of them didn't. The birds we see all around us came from a special group of very small dinosaurs!)

Scientists who study dinosaurs keep working to make new discoveries that will help us learn all we can about these amazing animals.

Parasaurolophus

ALLOSAURUS

(AL-uh-sawr-us)

Allosaurus means "leaping lizard." This dinosaur walked on two legs. Its long, heavy tail helped *Allosaurus* keep its balance.

Allosaurus was large and savage. It had a powerful neck, strong, wide-opening jaws, and pointed teeth. Its sharp claws were six inches long. *Allosaurus* used them to hold food — usually another dinosaur.

Approximate size relationship of an average, fully grown Allosaurus to a six-foot-tall adult:

HEIGHT: 16 feet (5m)
LENGTH: 39 feet (11.9m)
WEIGHT: 4 tons (4,000kg)
FOUND: Western U.S. (Utah)

◆ APATOSAURUS ◆

(ah-PAT-uh-sawr-us)

Apatosaurus means "deceptive lizard." This dinosaur had a long, long neck and a small head. Its brain was only as large as an adult's fist. This huge creature walked on four thick, sturdy legs that were shaped like an elephant's.

Apatosaurus was one of the biggest dinosaurs. Although it didn't have spikes, horns, or protective armor, it was able to defend itself with its long whip-like tail. *Apatosaurus* also kept safe by moving in herds. The babies were surrounded by a circle of adults that protected them from meat-eating dinosaurs.

HEIGHT: 15 feet (4.5m) at the hips
LENGTH: 75 feet (23m)
WEIGHT: 30 tons (30,000kg)

FOUND: Western Mexico,
Western U.S. (Montana)

Apatosaurus ate leaves and twigs. With its long neck, it could reach into the treetops to get the food it needed. This large animal needed lots of food. It probably had to spend most of the day eating.

Apatosaurus could eat fast because it didn't have to chew. This dinosaur swallowed small stones that helped grind up the plant food in its stomach.

Approximate size relationship of an average, fully grown Apatosaurus *to a six-foot-tall adult:*

◆ DEINONYCHUS ◆

(dye-NON-ik-us)

Deinonychus means "terrible claw." The name for this dinosaur comes from the curved claw on the back of each foot. *Deinonychus* had claws on all its toes and fingers. Claws were its most important weapon. They helped this meat-eater get food.

Deinonychus was small, quick, and aggressive. It could catch and hold other small dinosaurs with the claws on its hands, but most likely it attacked its prey with the claws on its feet.

HEIGHT: 6 feet (1.8m)
LENGTH: 10 feet (3m)
WEIGHT: 225 pounds (100kg)
FOUND: Western U.S. (Montana)

Deinonychus had strong jaws and sharp teeth. Its tail stood out stiffly from its body. That may have helped this dinosaur balance on one leg while kicking its victims with the other.

Deinonychus probably hunted in packs. That would have made it easier for this fierce, little creature to attack much larger dinosaurs.

Approximate size relationship of an average, fully grown Deinonychus *to a six-foot-tall adult:*

DIMETRODON

(dye-MET-ruh-don)

Dimetrodon means "teeth of two sizes." These teeth were long and sharp, which tells us *Dimetrodon* was a meat-eater.

Dimetrodon had a "sail" on its back that was about three feet high. This four-legged, dinosaur-like creature probably used its sail to scare away enemies or attract a mate.

Dimetrodon was not a dinosaur. It lived long before the first dinosaurs appeared.

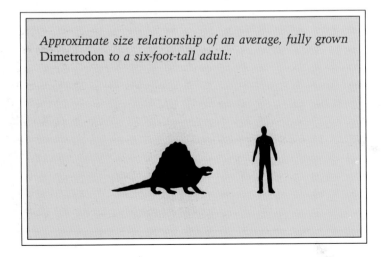

Approximate size relationship of an average, fully grown Dimetrodon *to a six-foot-tall adult:*

HEIGHT: 3 feet (0.9m)
LENGTH: 10 feet (3m)
WEIGHT: 300 pounds (136kg)
FOUND: Southwestern U.S. (Texas)

‹ PACHYCEPHALOSAURUS ›

(pak-ee-SEF-uh-lo-sawr-us)

Pachycephalosaurus means "thick-headed lizard." This dinosaur had a skull 20 times thicker than that of a human. Pachycephalosaurs might have fought each other by butting their thick skulls together, just as rams do.

Pachycephalosaurus wasn't one of the biggest dinosaurs and it wasn't one of the fastest. It had no spikes, horns, or sharp claws to use as weapons. Meat-eaters were dangerous enemies to *Pachycephalosaurus*.

This dinosaur used its good sense of smell and keen eyesight to avoid danger. Its thick skull may have been used like a battering ram to give *Pachycephalosaurus* some protection.

HEIGHT: 8 feet (2.4m)
LENGTH: 15 feet (4.5m)
WEIGHT: 2 tons (2,000kg)
FOUND: Western Canada,
Western U.S. (Wyoming)

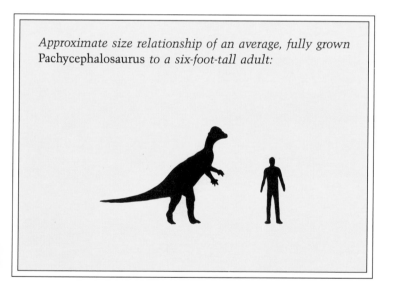

Approximate size relationship of an average, fully grown
Pachycephalosaurus *to a six-foot-tall adult:*

· PARASAUROLOPHUS ·

(par-ah-sawr-OL-uh-fus)

Parasaurolophus means "similar to Saurolophus," another crested dinosaur. The head crest of *Parasaurolophus* was a hollow tube about five-and-a-half-feet long.

Scientists are not sure what the crest was used for. They think that it might have helped this creature's sense of smell. It may also have been used like a trumpet. *Parasaurolophus* may have blown loud sounds through the tube to attract a mate or signal danger.

Parasaurolophus ate plants. It had hundreds of teeth for grinding up its food.

Approximate size relationship of an average, fully grown Parasaurolophus to a six-foot-tall adult:

HEIGHT: 16 feet (5m)
LENGTH: 30 feet (9m)
WEIGHT: 3 tons (3,000kg)
FOUND: Western Canada, Western U.S. (New Mexico, Utah)

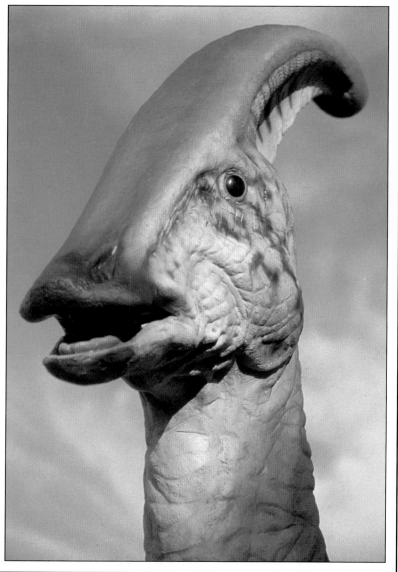

PTERANODON

(tair-AN-o-don)

Pteranodon means "winged and toothless." This flying creature was not a dinosaur, but it lived at the same time as the last dinosaurs.

Pteranodon had a long beak, and the male of the species had a long crest at the back of the head. With its wings stretched out, *Pteranodon* was wider than two cars.

This creature had bones that were light and hollow, and scientists believe it was a superb glider. *Pteranodon* fossils have been found more than 100 miles from shore.

Pteranodon ate fish that it caught in its beak as it flew over the sea. It had to swallow its food whole, as some seabirds do, because it had no teeth.

WINGSPAN: 27 feet (8.2m)

LENGTH: 8 feet (2.4m) from crest
to feet

WEIGHT: 35 pounds (16kg)

FOUND: Mid-western U.S. (Kansas)

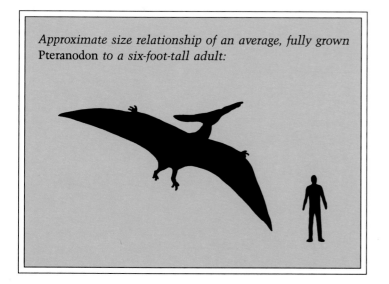

Approximate size relationship of an average, fully grown Pteranodon *to a six-foot-tall adult:*

◂ STEGOSAURUS ▸

(STEG-uh-sawr-us)

Stegosaurus means "plated lizard." Scientists aren't sure why *Stegosaurus* had plates on its back. Some think the plates worked to scare away enemies. Others believe they also helped control this dinosaur's body temperature.

Stegosaurus was a plant-eater that sliced up food with its teeth then swallowed without chewing. This four-legged creature moved slowly, and it had a tiny brain the size of a golf ball.

Approximate size relationship of an average, fully grown Stegosaurus to a six-foot-tall adult:

HEIGHT: 11 feet (3.3m) at hips
LENGTH: 27 feet (8.2m)
WEIGHT: 2 tons (2,000kg)
FOUND: Western U.S.
(Colorado, Utah, Wyoming)

TRICERATOPS

(try-SAIR-uh-tops)

Triceratops means "three-horned face." This dinosaur probably used its dangerous-looking horns to defend itself against meat-eating dinosaurs such as *Tyrannosaurus*.

Triceratops also had leathery skin and a large, bony frill at the back of its head that protected its neck and shoulders.

Even a young *Triceratops* had a frill and three horns, although these were not yet fully developed.

HEIGHT: 9 feet (2.9m)
LENGTH: 25 feet (7.5m)
WEIGHT: 7 tons (7,000kg)
FOUND: Western Canada,
Western U.S.
(Montana, Wyoming)

Underneath *Triceratops'* smallest horn was a sharp beak. This was used as a tool for cutting up the tough forest plants *Triceratops* ate.

Triceratops was not very tall, but it might have been able to eat from the treetops. This big beast was as large and heavy as an elephant, and it probably was able to push over small trees so it could eat the highest leaves and branches.

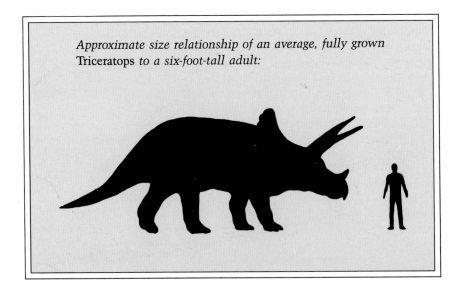

Approximate size relationship of an average, fully grown Triceratops *to a six-foot-tall adult:*

TYRANNOSAURUS

(tye-RAN-uh-sawr-us)

Tyrannosaurus means "tyrant lizard." With its knife-like teeth and huge jaws, *Tyrannosaurus* could tear off and swallow huge chunks of meat.

This fierce dinosaur had short arms that were only about two-and-a-half-feet long. The claws on its two fingers were long and sharp.

Tyrannosaurus was one of the last dinosaurs, and it was the largest of the meat-eaters. In fact, it is the largest known meat-eating animal ever to walk the earth.

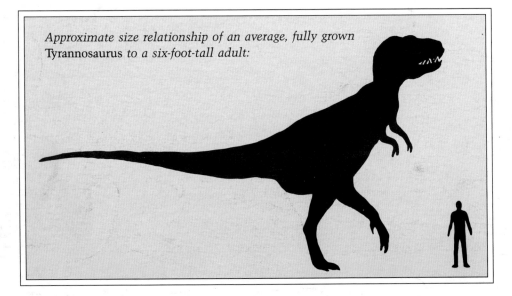

Approximate size relationship of an average, fully grown *Tyrannosaurus* to a six-foot-tall adult:

HEIGHT: 18 feet (5.6m)
LENGTH: 50 feet (15m)
WEIGHT: 7 tons (7,000kg)
FOUND: China, Western U.S. (Montana, Wyoming)

Allosaurus